D0102427

The Sprog Owner's Manual

CITY OF LIMERICK
C04241
PUBLIC LIBRARY

WARNING NOTE

Before acquiring a sprog, please read the following instructions

VERY CAREFULLY

The Sprog Owner's Manual

Babette Cole

A Tom Maschler Book
Jonathan Cape
London

How to Get

① Grow your own,

② adopt a ready-made one,

a Sprog

③ 'Rent-a-Sprog'

or ④ send off for one from a mail-order catalogue.

How to Recognise a Good Sprog

How to Recognise a Bad Sprog

Fuel (or What Sprogs Eat)

Good sprog fuel
(healthy)

Bad sprog fuel
(unhealthy)

Fuel Processing for Body

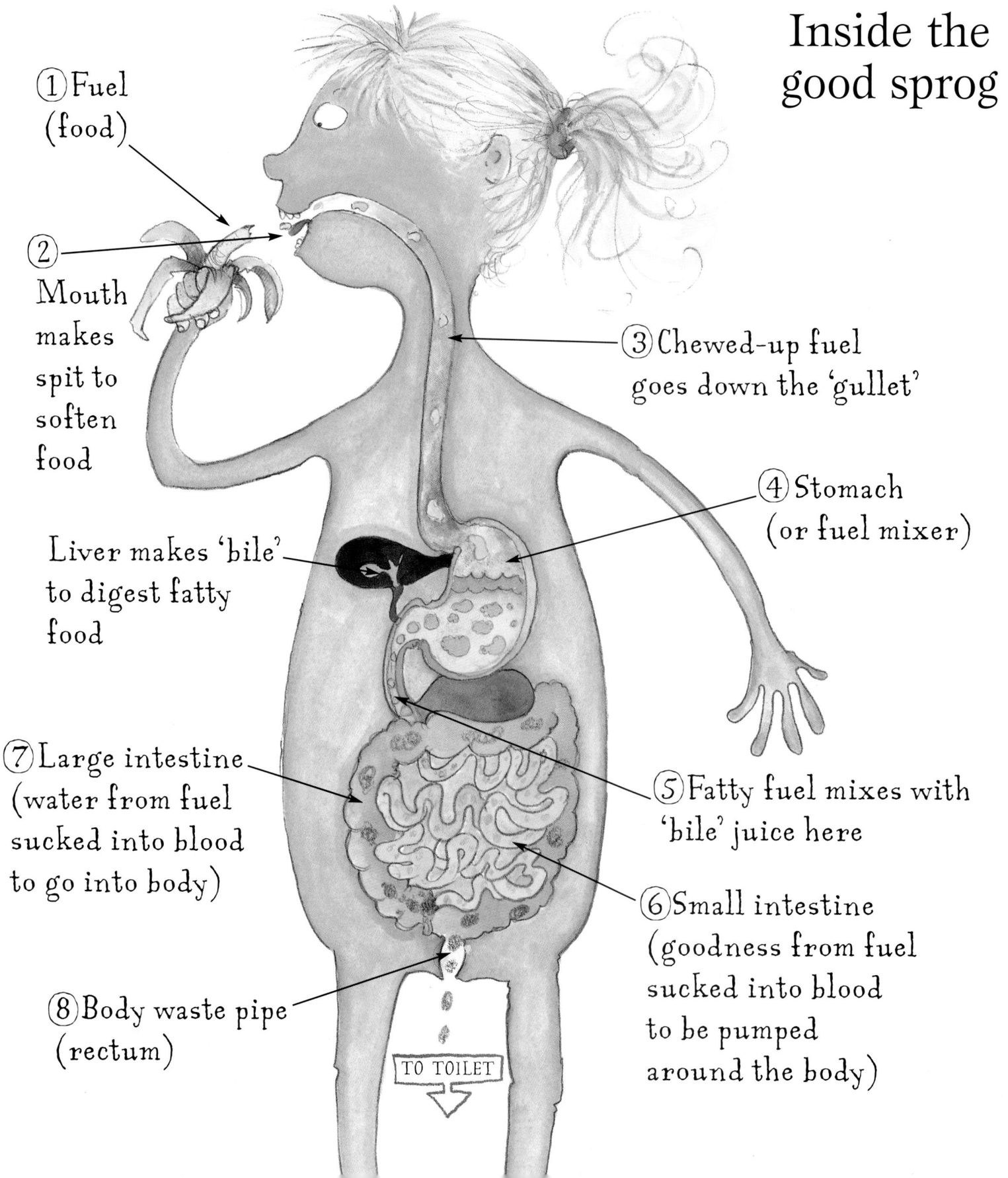

Performance (or Digestion)

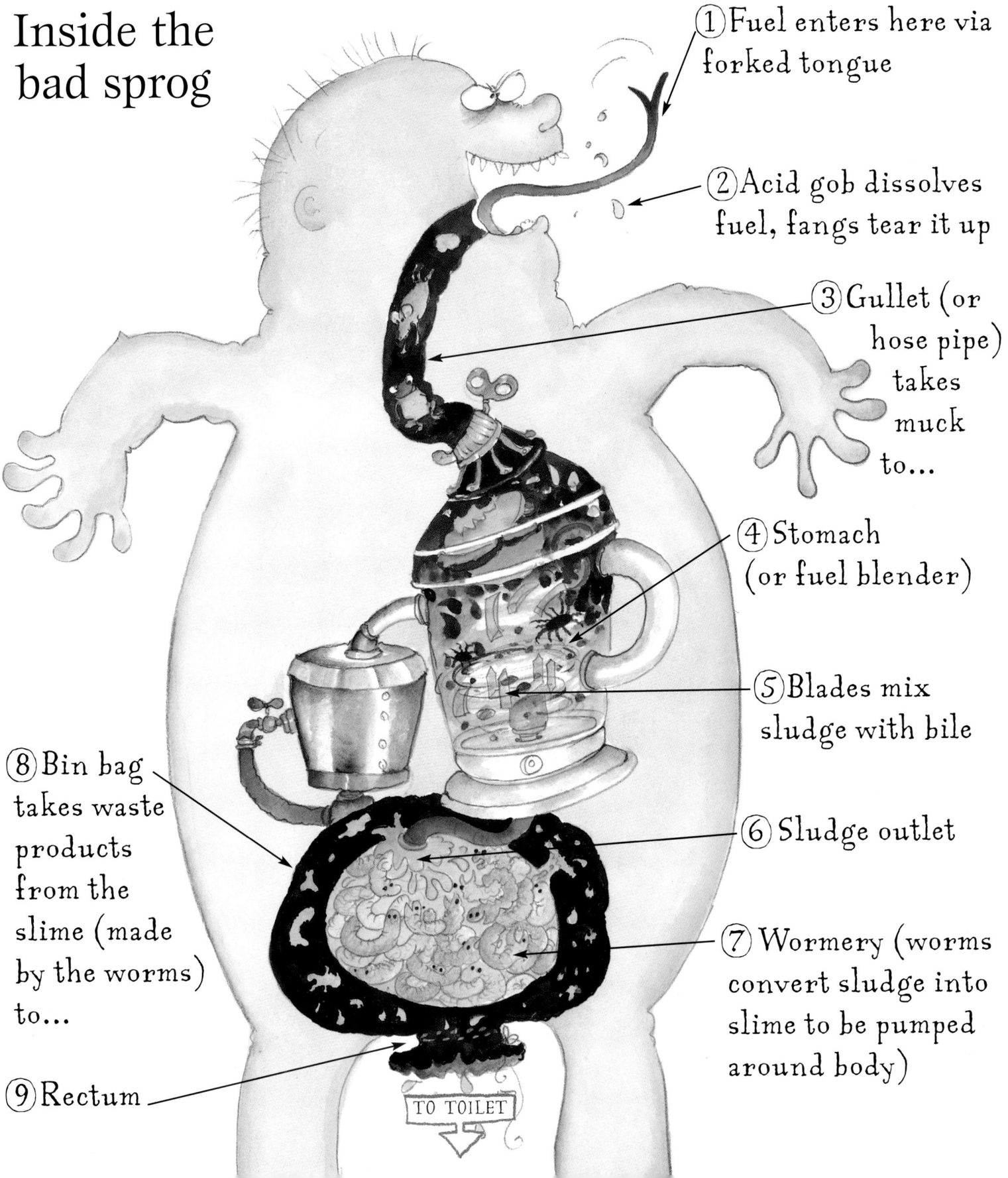

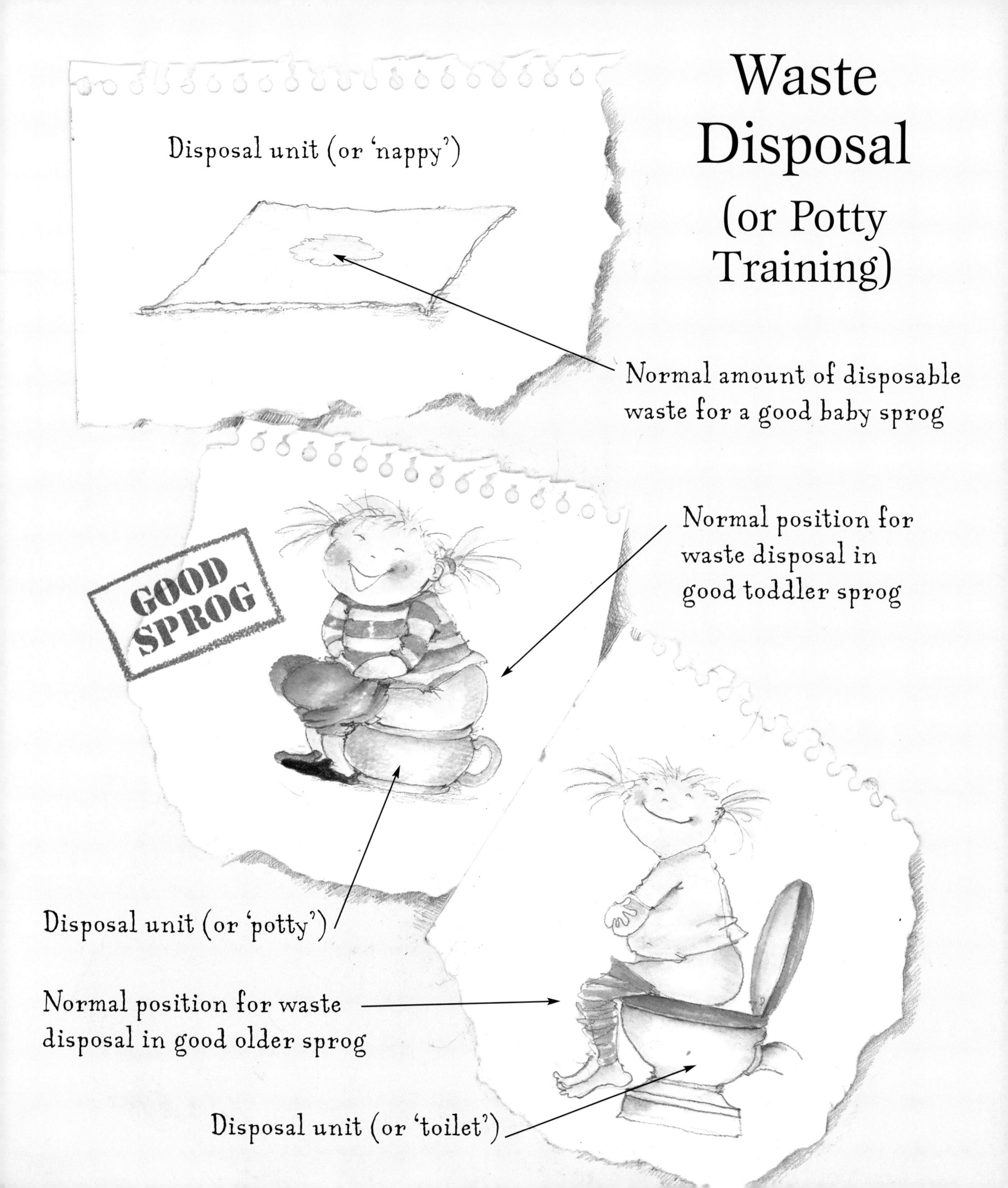
Waste Disposal
(or Potty Training)
Disposal unit (or 'nappy')
Normal amount of disposable waste for a good baby sprog
GOOD SPROG
Normal position for waste disposal in good toddler sprog
Disposal unit (or 'potty')
Normal position for waste disposal in good older sprog
Disposal unit (or 'toilet')

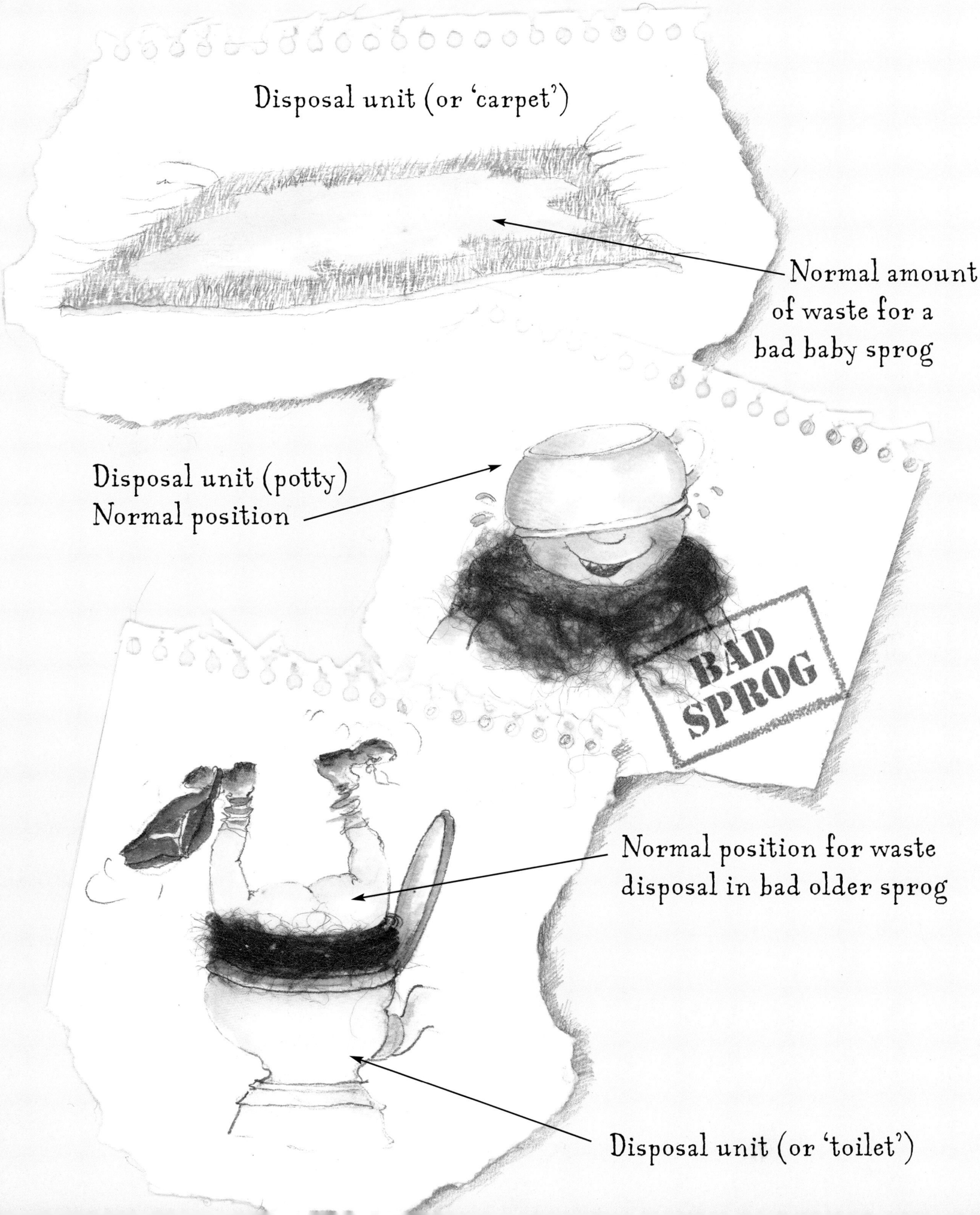
Disposal unit (or 'carpet')
Normal amount of waste for a bad baby sprog
Disposal unit (potty)
Normal position
BAD SPROG
Normal position for waste disposal in bad older sprog
Disposal unit (or 'toilet')

Air Intake (Breathing Equipment)

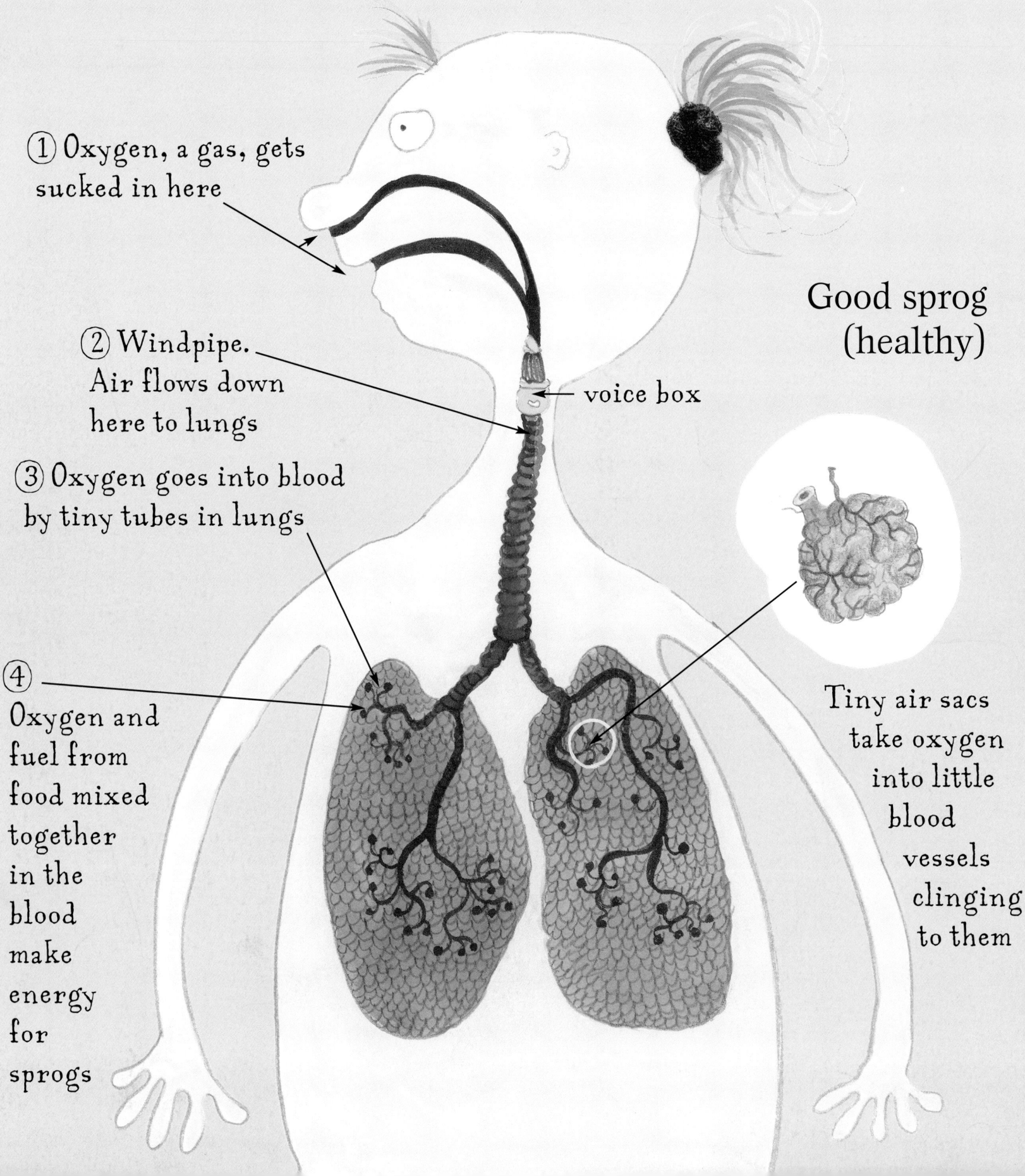

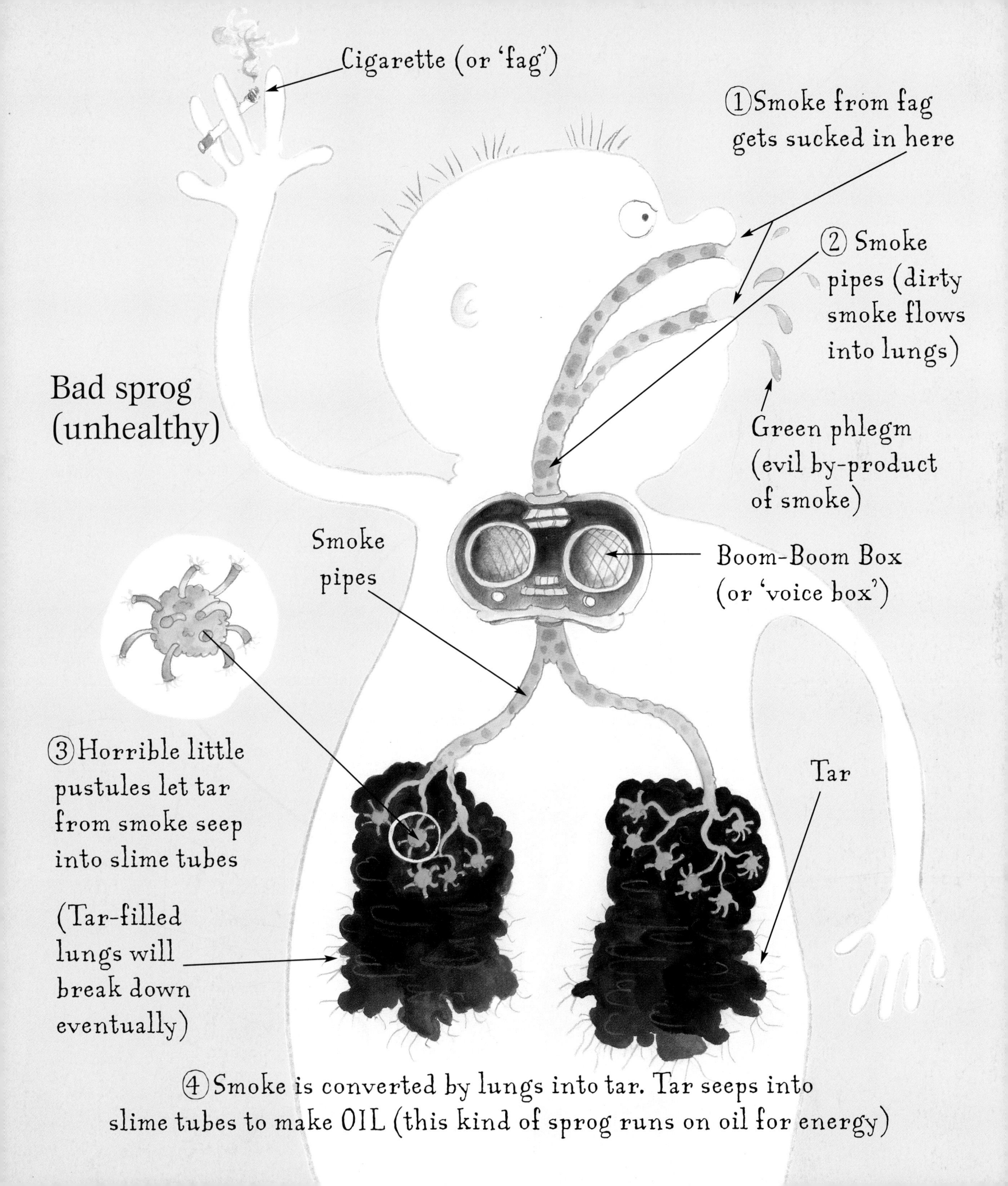
Cigarette (or 'fag')
① Smoke from fag gets sucked in here
② Smoke pipes (dirty smoke flows into lungs)
Bad sprog (unhealthy)
Green phlegm (evil by-product of smoke)
Smoke pipes
Boom-Boom Box (or 'voice box')
③ Horrible little pustules let tar from smoke seep into slime tubes
Tar
(Tar-filled lungs will break down eventually)
④ Smoke is converted by lungs into tar. Tar seeps into slime tubes to make OIL (this kind of sprog runs on oil for energy)

Sprog Pumping System

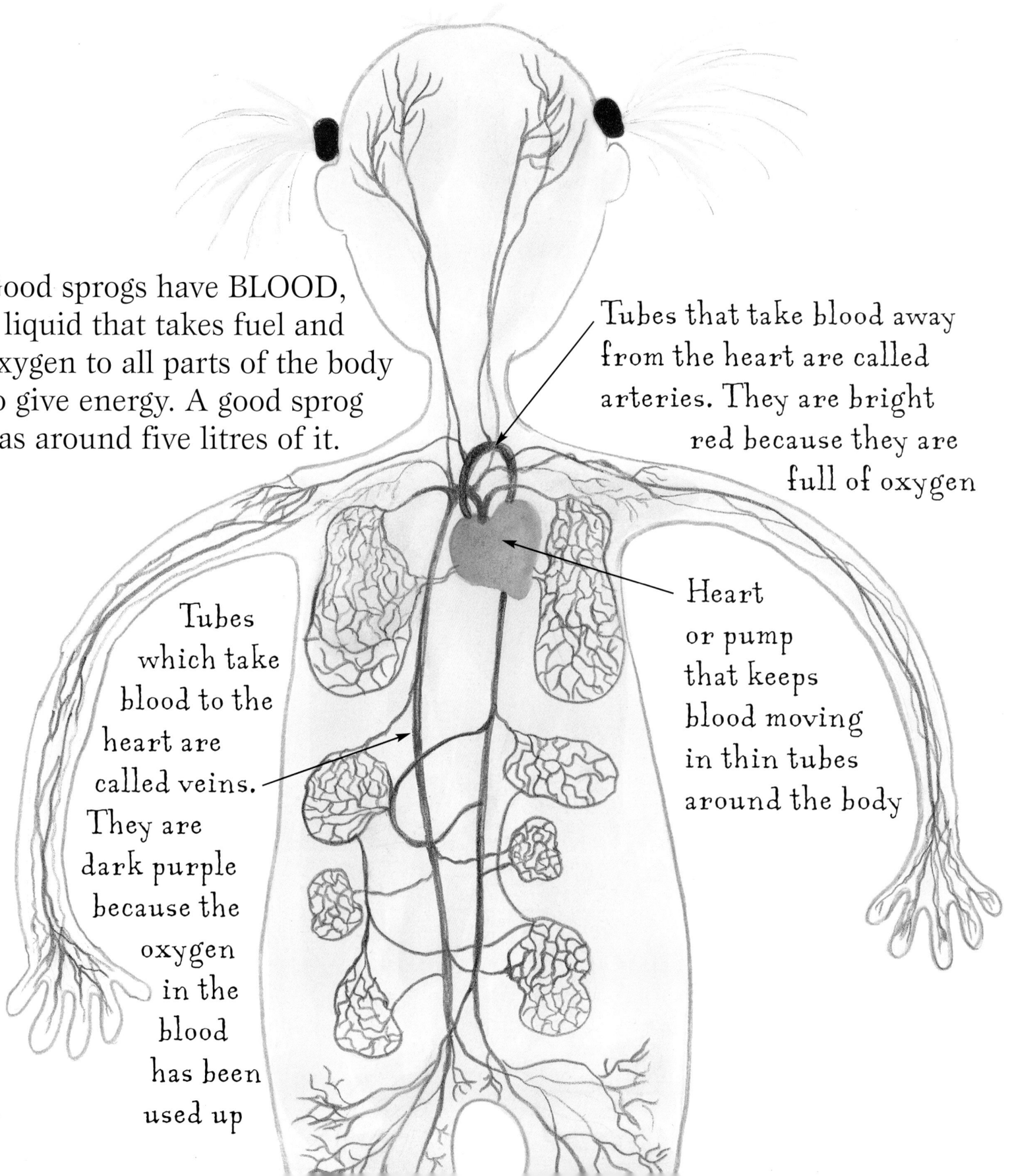

Bad sprogs have OIL, a liquid that takes tar and slime around its body to give energy.

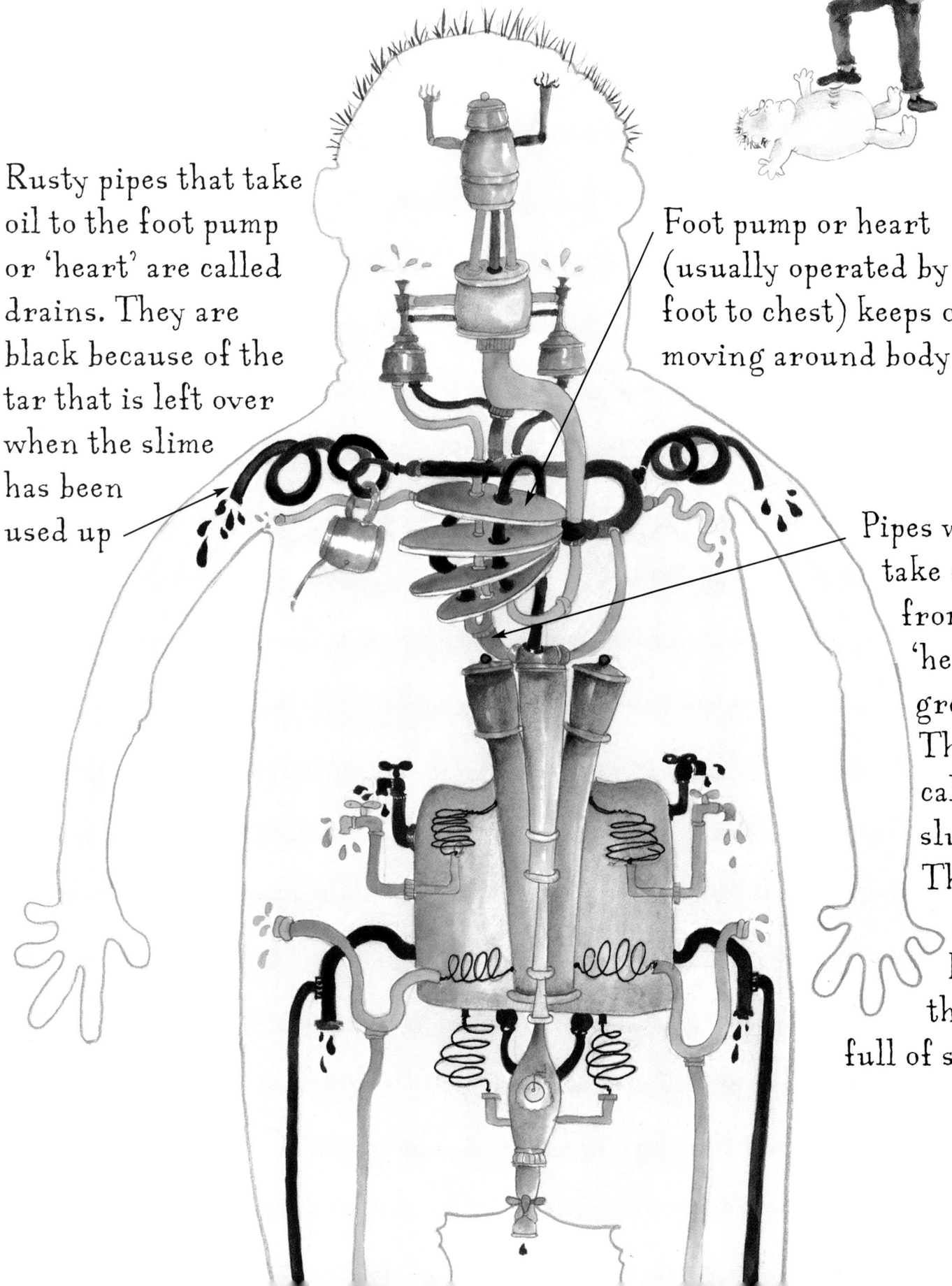

Framework and Fittings

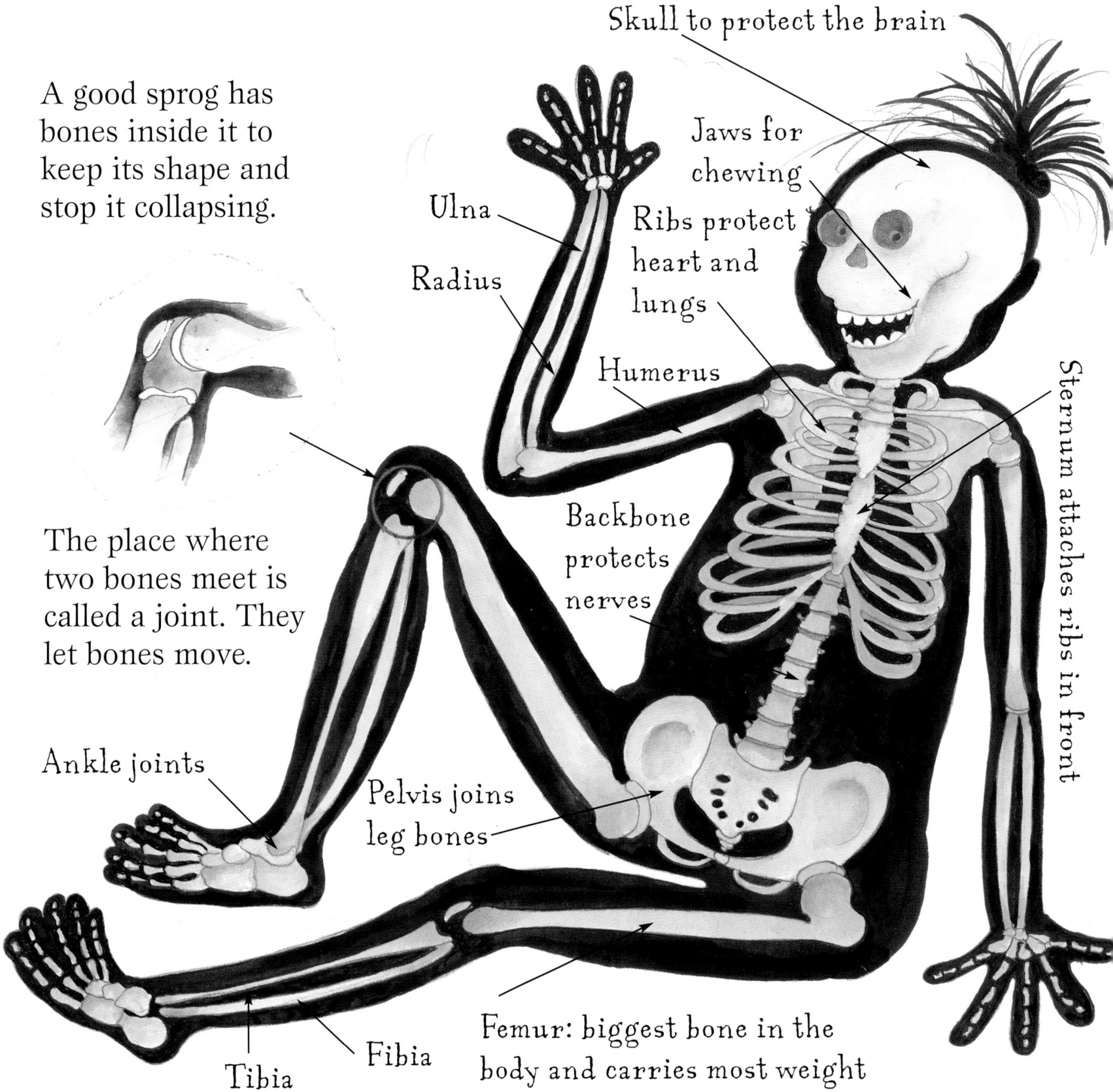

(or How Sprogs Move)

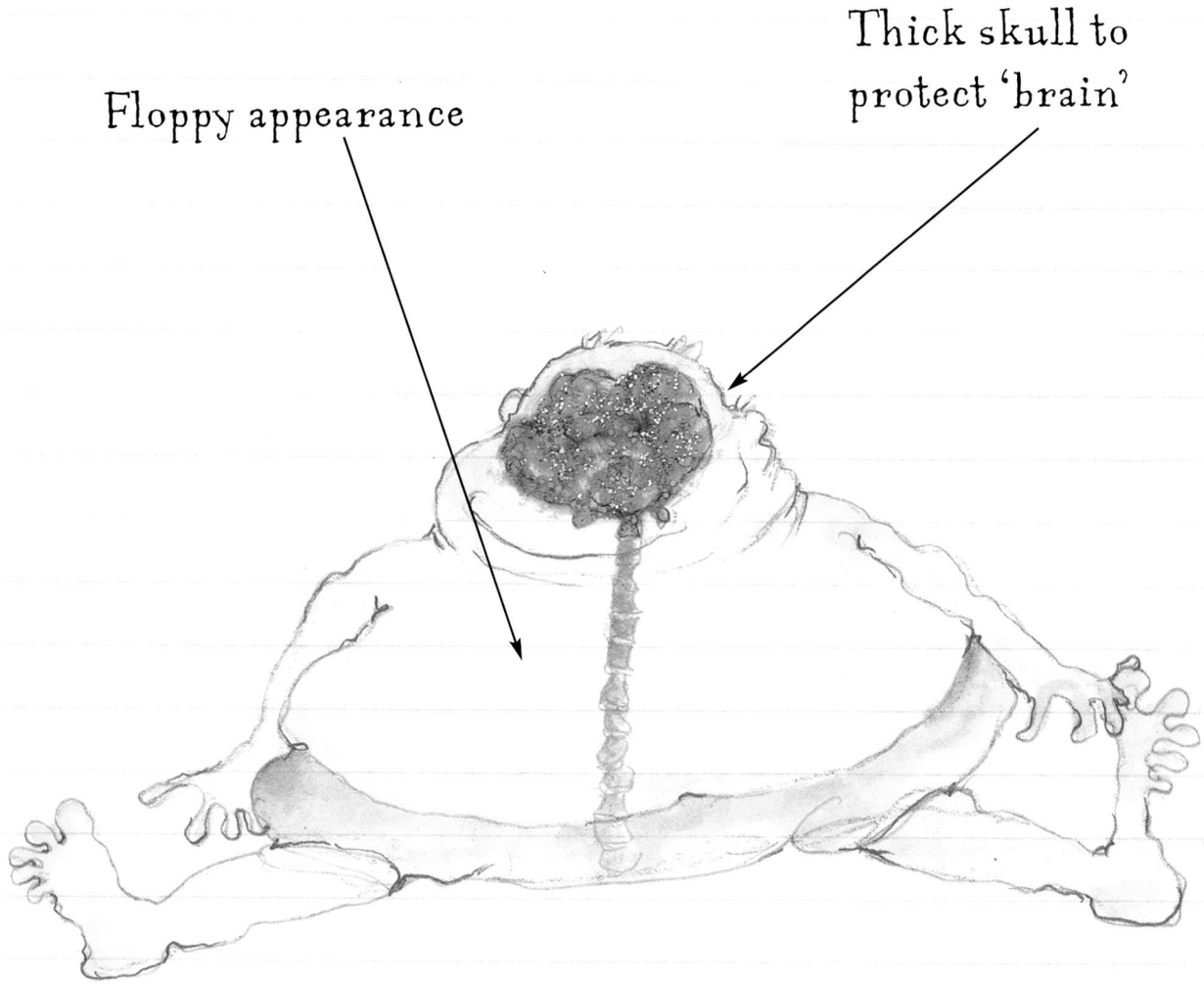

Avoid this kind of sprog – it has no bones!

Suspension and Steering

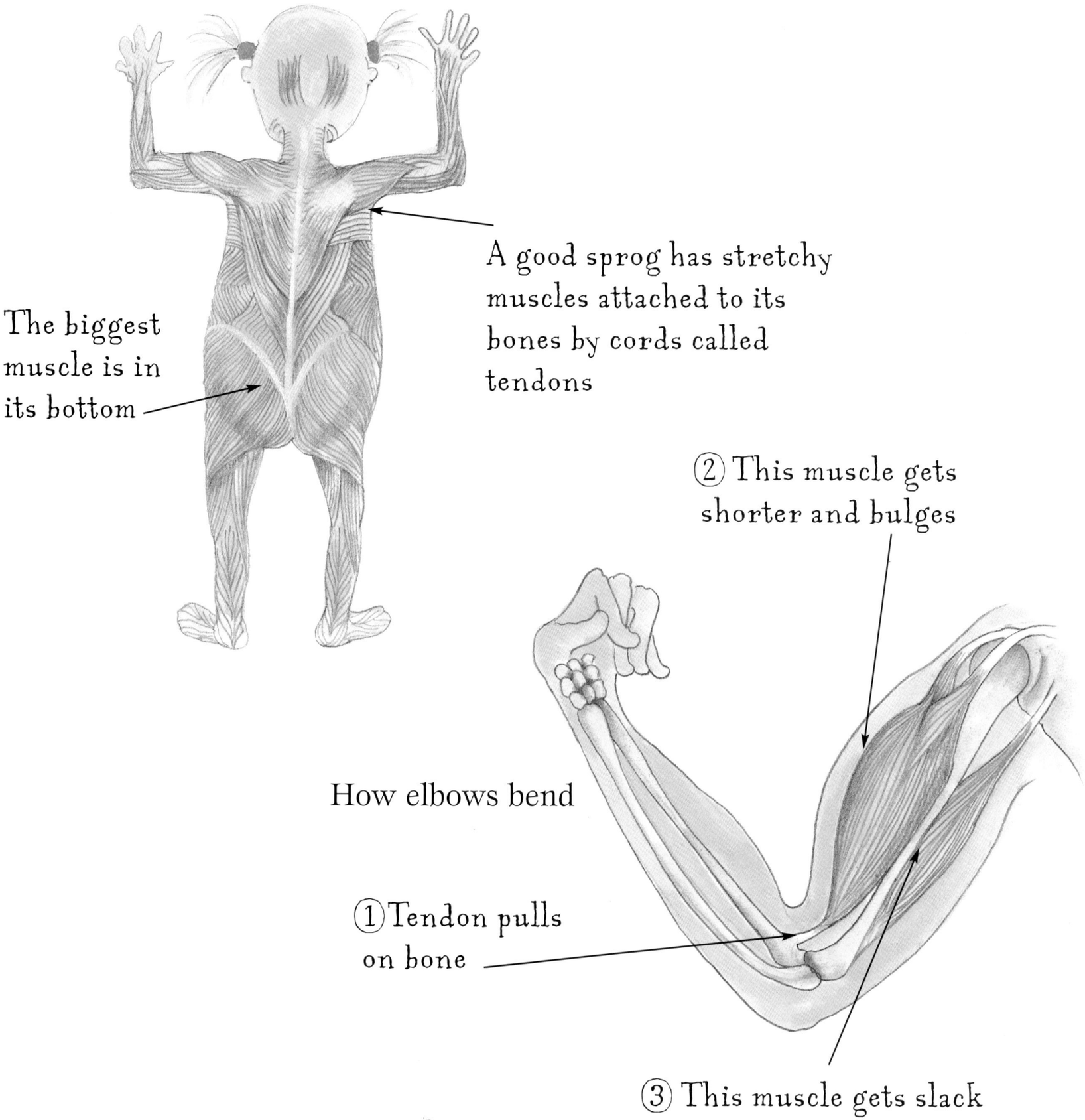

(How Sprogs Move, continued)

C04241

As bad sprogs have no bones they have to be pumped up regularly with SPROG GEL.

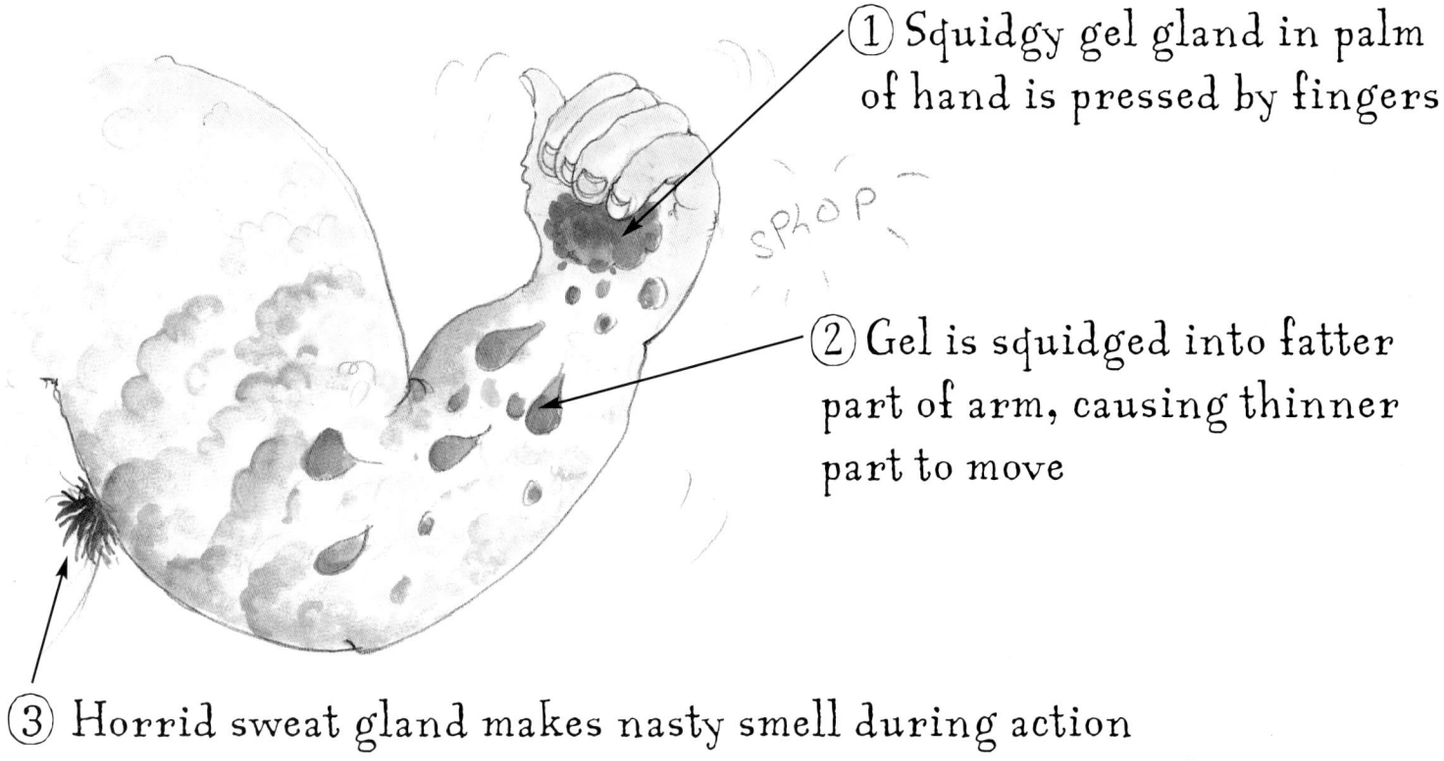

Central Computer or Brain

Located inside the head, the 'brain' controls the whole body.
DO NOT attempt 'Home Mechanics' or brain swapping…

because a ‘bad’ sprog brain in a ‘good’
sprog can have dreadful side effects!

Wiring
(or How the Brain Sends Messages to the Body)

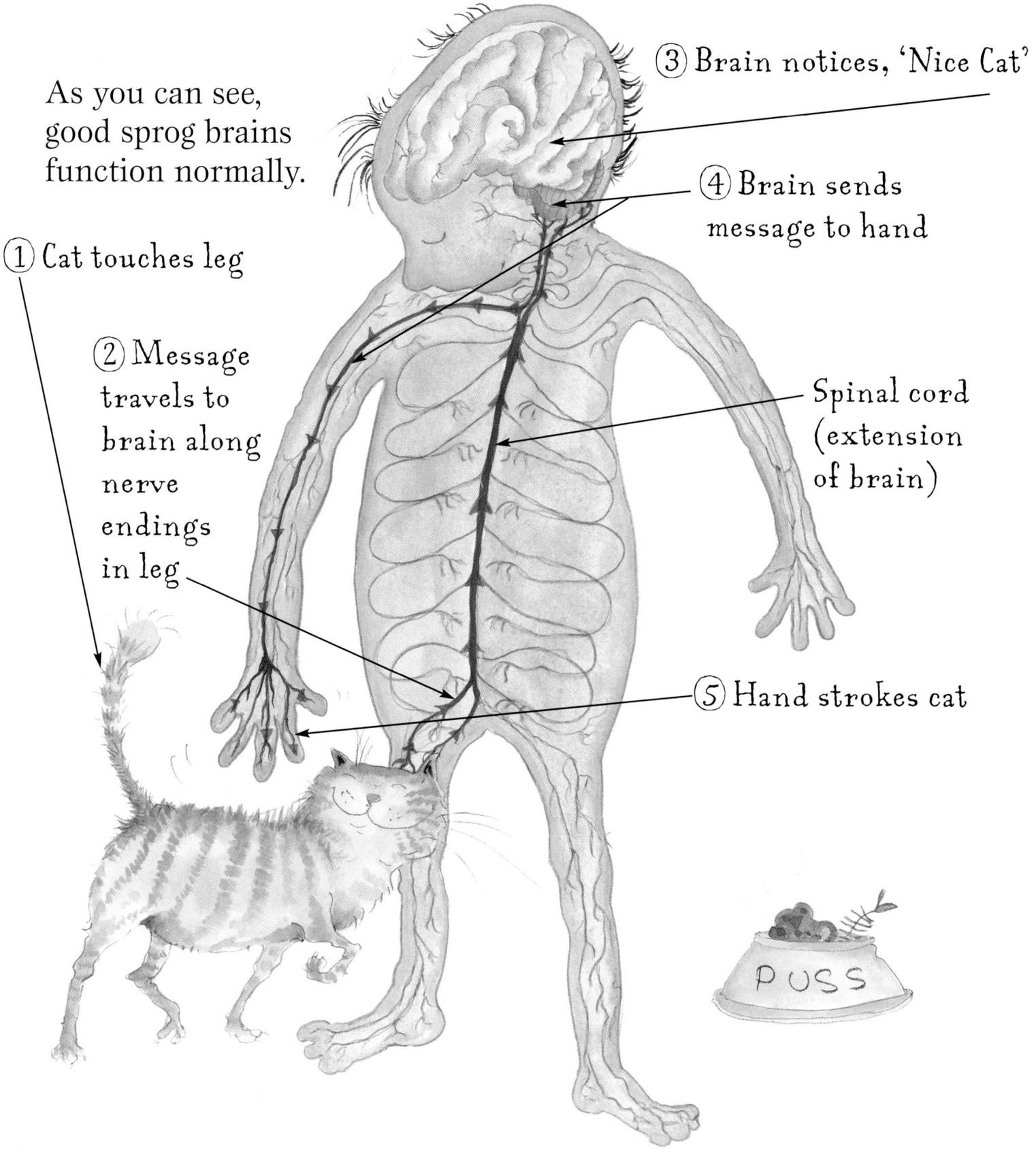

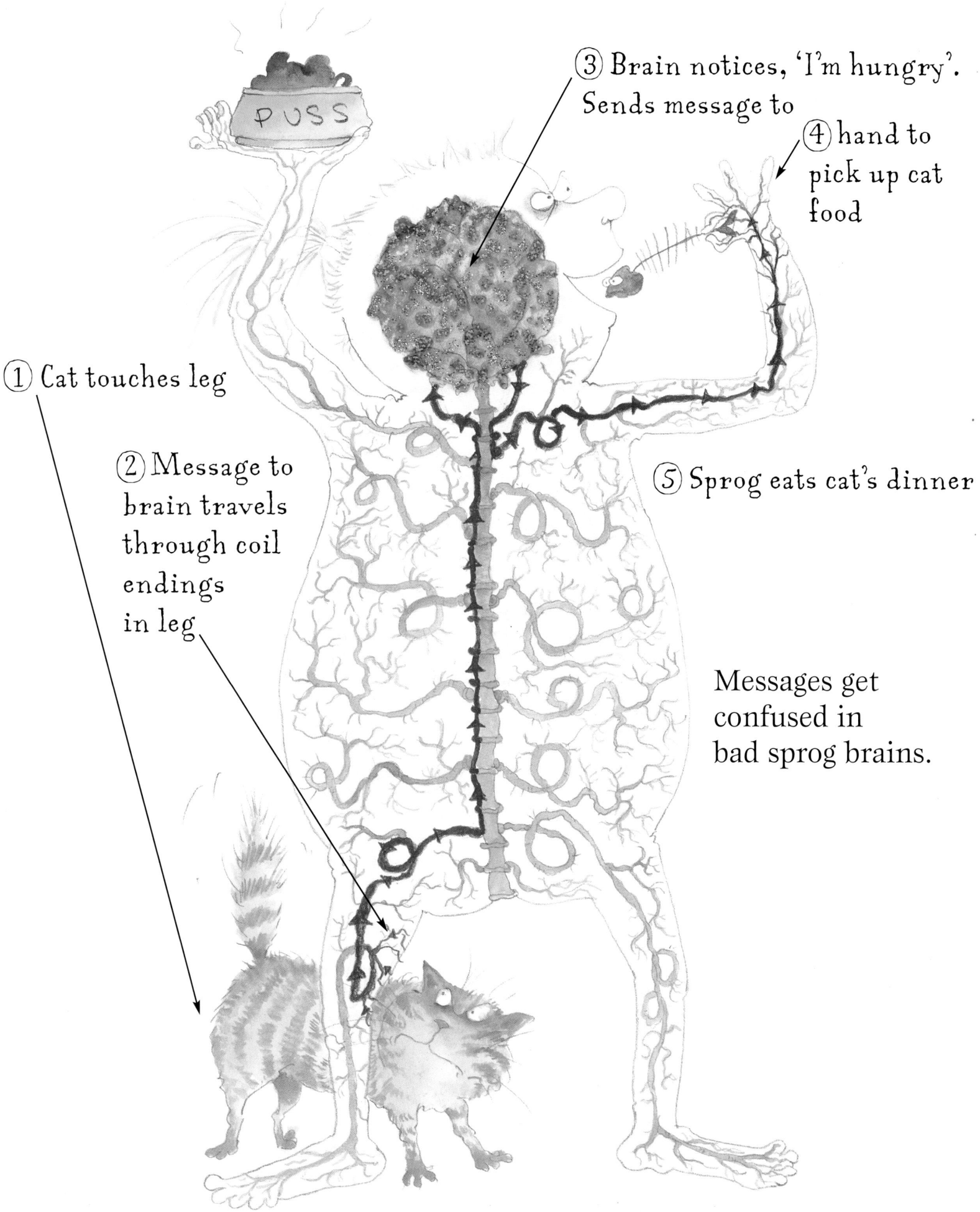
PUSS
③ Brain notices, 'I'm hungry'. Sends message to
④ hand to pick up cat food
① Cat touches leg
② Message to brain travels through coil endings in leg
⑤ Sprog eats cat's dinner
Messages get confused in bad sprog brains.

Headlights
(or How Sprogs See)

Blown-up cross section of a good sprog headlight or eye.

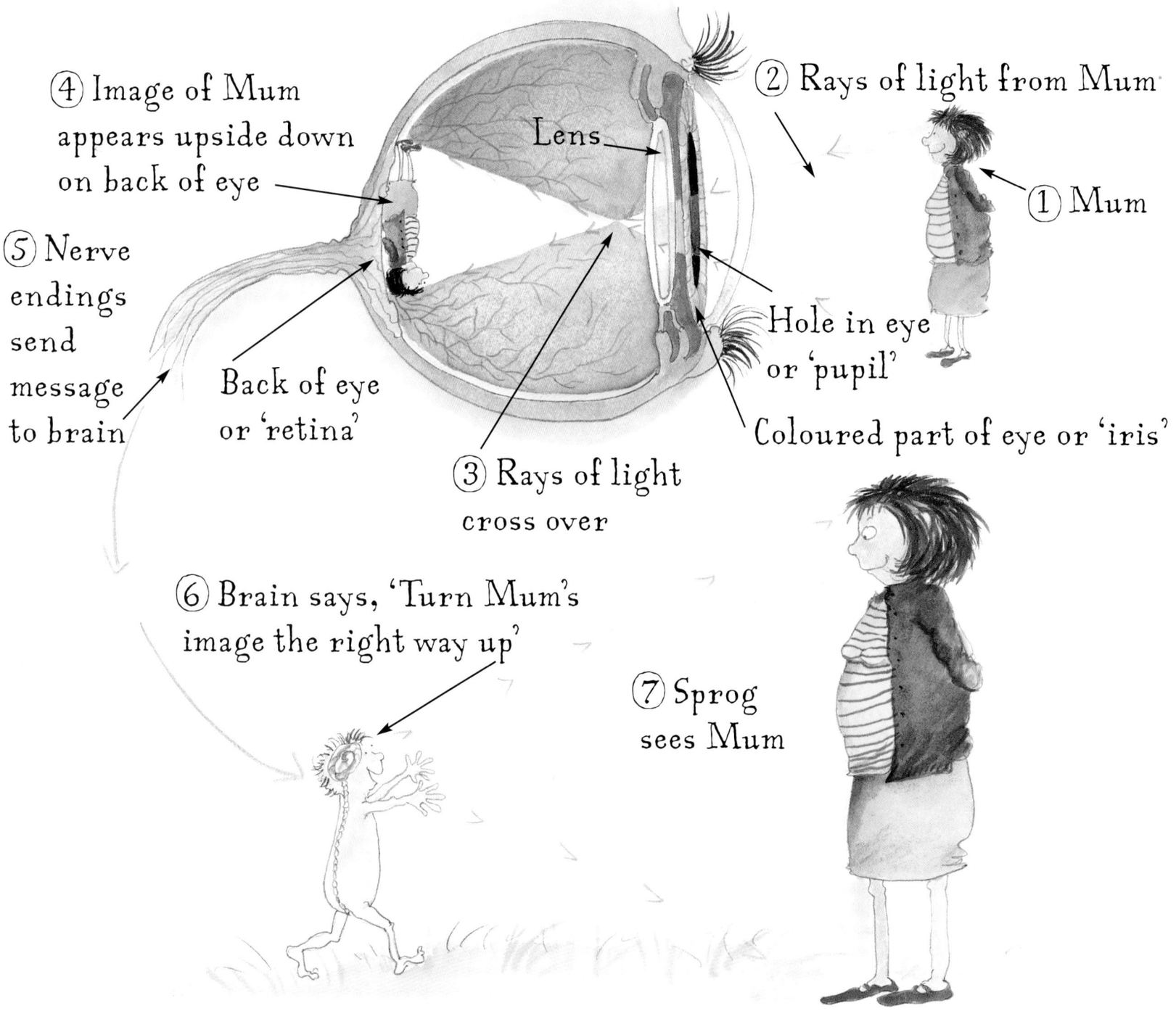

Blown-up cross section of a bad sprog headlight or eye.

Earbox (or

Cross section of good sprog ear

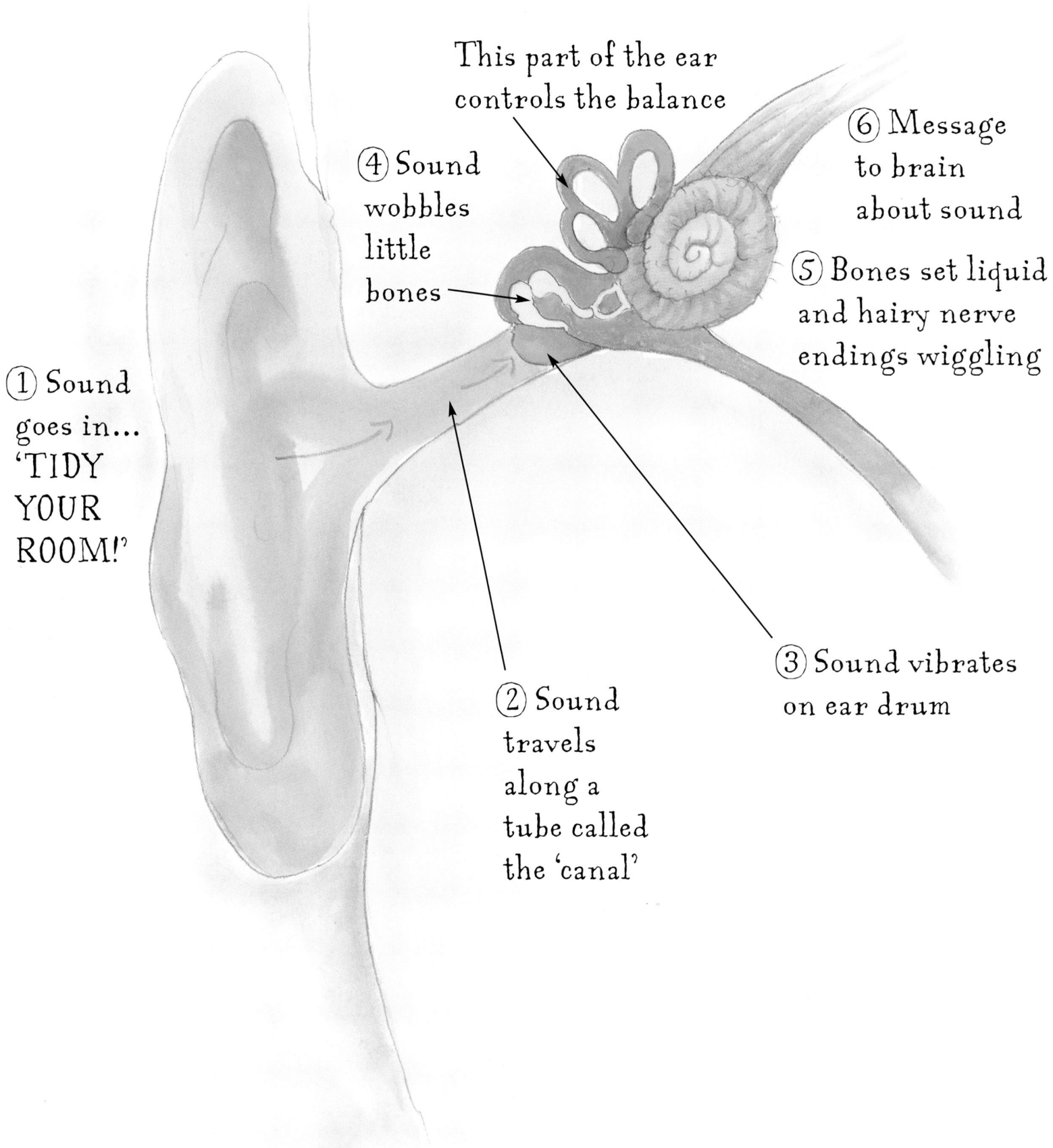

How Sprogs Hear)

Cross section of bad sprog ear

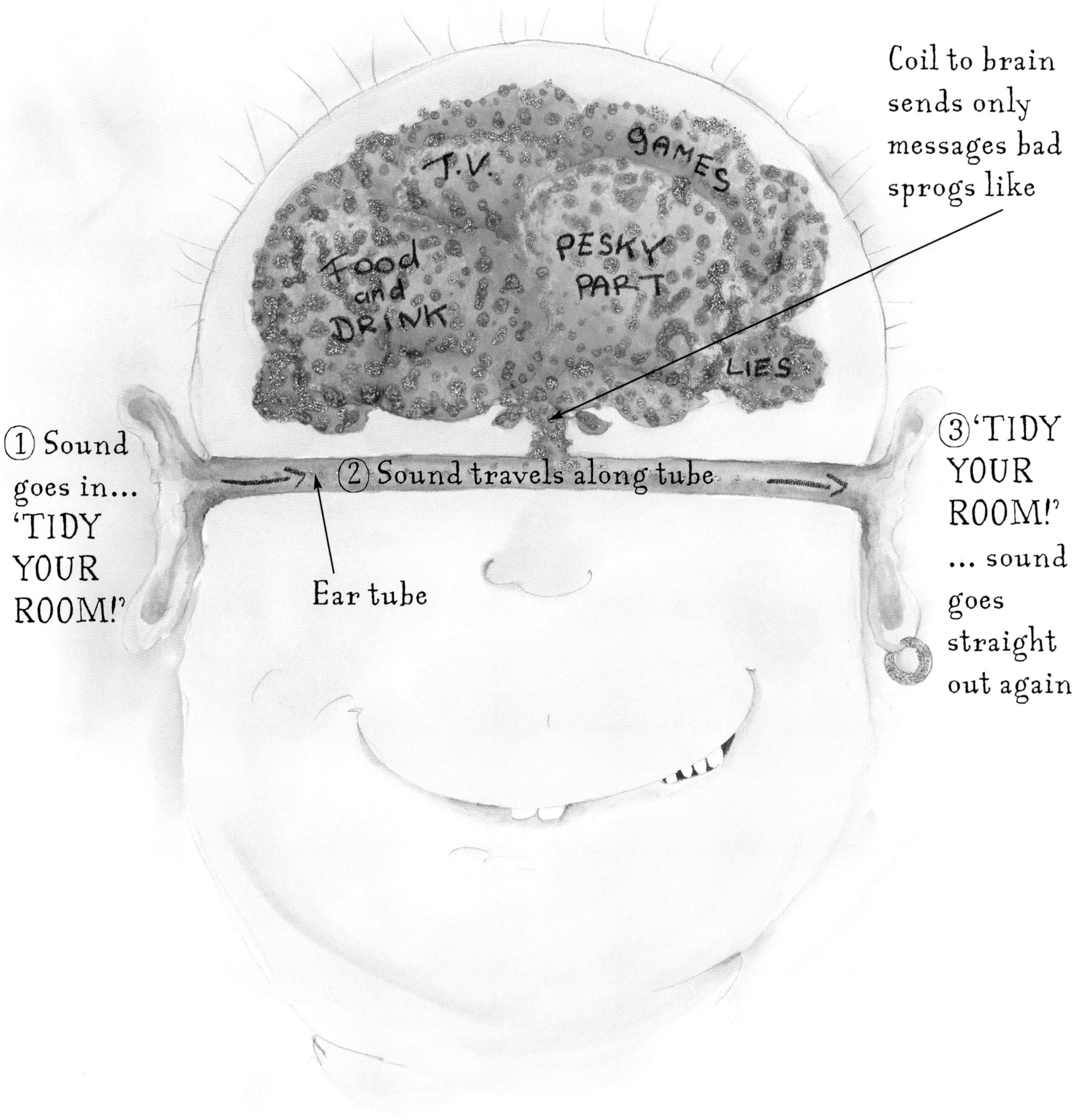

General Maintenance
(or How to Make Your Sprog Last)

① Do not leave a good sprog out in the rain

② Change nappy and wash regularly

③ Store in a safe, warm place at night

① Do leave bad sprogs out in the rain as they like to rust

② Do not attempt to wash or change nappy

③ Store in a safe place at night

What to do in case of

For a
good sprog
call an
ambulance.

Emergency Breakdown

Not much you can do in the case of a bad one.

① Think very carefully
before acquiring a sprog
② Remember a sprog is for ever...
...not just for Christmas!
Better
be certain
I make a
good one

Helpful Hints for Future Owners

CITY OF LIMERICK
04241
PUBLIC LIBRARY

For Georgie - a good sprog?

THE SPROG OWNER'S MANUAL
A JONATHAN CAPE BOOK 0 224 06487 8

Published in Great Britain by Jonathan Cape,
an imprint of Random House Children's Books

This edition published 2004

1 3 5 7 9 10 8 6 4 2

Copyright © Babette Cole, 2004

The right of Babette Cole to be identified as the author of this work has been asserted
in accordance with the Copyright, Designs and Patents Act 1988.

All rights reserved.

RANDOM HOUSE CHILDREN'S BOOKS
61-63 Uxbridge Road, London W5 5SA
A division of The Random House Group Ltd
RANDOM HOUSE AUSTRALIA (PTY) LTD
20 Alfred Street, Milsons Point, Sydney,
New South Wales 2061, Australia
RANDOM HOUSE NEW ZEALAND LTD
18 Poland Road, Glenfield, Auckland 10, New Zealand
RANDOM HOUSE (PTY) LTD
Endulini, 5A Jubilee Road, Parktown 2193, South Africa

THE RANDOM HOUSE GROUP Limited Reg. No. 954009
www.**kids**at**randomhouse**.co.uk
www.babette-cole.com

A CIP catalogue record for this book is available from the British Library.

Printed in Singapore